Atlas: Weight of the World

& other poems

by Jessica Tomlin

For my grandma:

*The one who keeps me grounded,
whilst always letting me soar.*

Contents

Atlas: Weight of the World .... **Page 7**

Apollo: The Haunting of the Prophet .... **Page 10**

Echo: Echo .... **Page 13**

Eris: Discordia's Reprisal .... **Page 15**

Persephone: Her Seasons .... **Page 17**

Eurydice: Misplaced Trust .... **Page 19**

The Fates: Atropos' Anguish .... **Page 23**

Hephaestus: The Cremation of Control .... **Page 25**

Tele-who? .... **Page 28**

Tartarus .... **Page 31**

End Notes .... **Page 32**

Atlas: Weight of the World

Strike me
with a thunderbolt of familiar fury
drench me
in acidic rain
crush me
with the falling sky.

Zeus

These shoulders
bear the weight of the world
the Heavens and Earth
they feel like Hell.
These bones
splinter and pierce the skin
but never falter beneath their load.
These eyes
they blur from the falling sweat
metallic with blood.

Zeus

Won't you free me now?
Dismiss these hundred hands
and let me
crawl away, cracked and weightless

back to my daughters,
understand the penance
was enough.

My Hesperides

Alight in the enclosing darkness of the setting sun
whole
as the Golden Apples guarded
I hear
your songs when the sleep seizes me.

My Pleiades

All six doves rising with the sails
and Merope
my missing child, wherever you soar now
I catch
glimpses of white wings hiding in my clouded sight.

My Hyades

Encouraging laments with each rainfall sent
stop
withhold those compassionate cries
and shine
in the head of Taurus, my raining constellation.

Zeus?

Now Mount Atlas
pierces the heavens with snowy peaks
I ask him
take me when you go
crushed and weak
I will let you haul me up through the night.

Apollo: The Haunting of the Prophet

Naivety would presume her beauty
bears no consequence,
but a frame like hers
captured my unwavering admiration.

Like Circe had cast her spells
and Eros had aimed his arrows
straight at my crotch,
I tried to foster her affection
with gifts of prophecy:
a flair for foretelling her future
but blind to her demise.

When entering the unknown with someone new,
tracks must be covered,
preparations made
and in the event of emergency,
certain exits built.

But with her dire lack of gratitude,
my raven cried fury and impelled my hand
to burn holes in her gift,
to seal it closed with a shrewd curse.

Despite the sincerity of her
predictions,

she would be presumed a
fabricator:
a furtive liar.

Cassandra's despair did not kindle,
did not ignite,
engulf,
did not destroy.
She found her gift, hidden beneath the curse,
allowing her to touch the future
with wayward eyes.

The prophecy I sought was stronger than hers
and her hapless demise
approached her unaware.

Her murderer:
Clytemnestra – axe and fury in tow
and not, of course, by these clean hands of my own.

A boy crying wolf:
'Danger, danger, danger lies ahead'
I can still hear her cries echoed by howls.
Is it a boy crying wolf, or
perhaps her mother's barks,
condemned to a hound?

Lachesis rises from behind the mountain,

draped in thread,
cut sharp and straight;
she snaps at my hands,
it was not her time.
Followed by Atropos, gold scissors glinting in the light,
it was not the Gods' way!
I say when, Apollo, I break the tie!
And finally, Cassandra herself,
ethereal and ever further out of my reach.

She taunts me incessantly, weaving lies amongst
supposed prophecies,
my suggested demise
at the hands of Drago?
My laugh echoes around the mountain:
an immortal God like I?

I try to walk away, trip on Lachesis thread
as Cassandra's final words fly by on the westerly wind.
But, what of Zeus?
The wind rises, roars, the threads bind my ankles,
Cassandra, come back, what of Zeus?

Echo: Echo

'is anyone here?'
'here'

Won't someone come by,
utter something profound?

Isn't that how rumours ignite?
A movement begins?

I fear my brain may rot inside my skull
'here'

Here I am, Narcissus,
floating from branch to leaf

silently screaming
can you hear me?

Here I can only talk with the trees

They call to the wind
who-shh

and I hush them
shh

Then, 'are you still there
or have you gone away?'
and I, 'away'.

Narcissus – with charcoal eyes
that once lit fires,
now dull and darting
found himself in shallow water.

No compassion lies in these sons of river-gods
and fountain-nymphs,
they slip from you like the rivers of their father's,
carelessly carrying you with them.

The wind soothed the trees and she called back
as I hushed them all

to watch the man I loved
drown trying to drink himself.

Eris: Discordia's Reprisal

You will find me on the battlefield
picking crusted blood from the palms
of my hands,
where the remnants of humans
have long since decayed.

With eyes of oil-slick black,
I scan the field for the
wandering spirits:
wailing, they wonder
why why why

and I bear my blackened teeth:
a sullied smile
with pointed canines,
parading blood-coated flesh and human hair.

'Eris, Eris
no, you shall not come
to the wedding of Thetis
and Peleus'.

Shall I not?

'Eris, Eris
you are a menace,

discordant reveller in rivalry.
No, you shall not come,
Eris'.

But please, Thetis and Peleus
and delicate guests,
you will call me
Discordia:
professional reveller of rivalry,
seeker of dissension
creator of contention.

Eris is far from here now,
her ashes scattered on the battlefield,
at home with the other querulous souls.
No, Discordia slithers in her place.

Both yourselves and your guests
should tread warily now,
for this is my reprisal.

Persephone: Her Seasons

Here come the supple shoots
of spring, the enkindling
of colour, the revival
of life, splintering through
the arid and bleak earth
and escaping into the season.

Helios drives the chariot
in Apollo's wake,
with idle hands and wandering gazes,
aureola crowning him,
burning his scalp and
sinking through his skin.

He drives from River Okeanos,
lying like dark, arcane veins
west to the land of the Hesperides,
sulking in the shadows
Apollo casts.

But here comes Persephone,
pale green robes draped like liquid
over curves and contours
beneath fervid red hair,
sown with petals of powder blue.

Her hands reach out and up,
pale stems shooting from her head:
ablaze.
Her legs move slow,
breaking ties with the roots of the Underworld.
She tilts back her head,
petals falling by her thin, worn heels.

'Join me Thea, let your light
emanate and here,
Triptolemos, teach the young buds
to unfold,
for before long, Hades will call,
Autumn will fall
and I shall shrink
and shrivel
with the shrubs and trees,
falling like lifeless leaves
back to the Underworld
back to Hades
to wait for Spring again.

Eurydice: Misplaced Trust

In the tombs of Tartarus
where walls of severed skulls
line endless flights of fetid stairs,
intense with the stench of sour flesh,
scorched from crumbling bones,
I lie in an eternal wait.

But my tale first begins near the valley of Tempe,
lying like a scar in floral flesh
where the River Peneus
slithers down like the dirty hands of Aristaeus
which slid up my legs
in pursuit of my purity.

In my frenetic escape from clambering hands,
I stepped on a snake
whose venom fled through my veins
and coiled around my heart
until it stopped
dead.

Then Tartarus became my home,
the shrieks and cries: a lullaby
to which I never slept,
until Orpheus came
from above

trilling a tune of rescue.

Through the passage that opens at
Aornum in Thesprotis,
he appeared, skin clear
and hair clean.
He was day rising
in this constant night.

His talents and irrefutable charm
enticed the ferryman
the Dog Cerberus
the three judges of the dead
with those persuasive,
plaintive lyre songs;
they briefly thawed
Hades' unyielding heart.

In his moments of mercy,
he called to Orpheus:

'*Stray my kingdom of darkness
but stay with eyes stagnant on the sun,
never turn back
until you reach the safe light of the day
for if you do, you fail,
Eurydice will forever be gone*'.

With fleeting faith, I followed Orpheus
to the very mouth of my home,
where the darkness began to fade.
But my Orpheus, effete with awe,
temptation teasing his head to turn,
glanced back to see if I was still in tow
and it was then

I felt the familiar caress of snakes
wrapping around my legs, my arms
my waist;
they writhed and tensed,
crushing bones and spirit,
dragging me back

to Tartarus
to Hades' opening arms
and to my death.

Beyond the hiss of fire
I am sure I still hear the buzz
of the bees I once kept,
still see glimpses of flames
and mistake them for sun.

Misplaced faith in a God with charm,
for that foolishness I paid the price of freedom,
reveries of strong arms and rescue die

and hope no longer lies with man or son.

Once the motion of revenge sets in,
rarely can it be undone.

The Fates: Atropos' Anguish

With solemn severity,
these hands
these trembling hands
clasp the shears of life and death.

At times they threaten to
slip in the sweat and drop but
my faltering grip never yields
as my own fate is ever advancing.

I fall to my knees as
the old man's face lifts from
his trembling hands.
His eyes animate with dew of life:
the potential years that would lie ahead.

But Lachesis chose his lot in life:
its quality, its purpose, its length.
A fair man: old, but with years left to give.

And yet the thread of life
that Clotho spun
has reached its point
of death.

My face creases

like plains of Poseidon's desert land
and these leaden eyes of mine
wash streams through the cracks
to be met by the cool hand
of the man.

'Cut the thread, Atropos,
I have already forgiven you.
It is alright,
it is done.'

The salt of my tears dry on his fingertips.

I hover the shears by his thread -
marked black
and with still, dry hands,
cut.

'But-'

Hephaestus: The Cremation of Control

It was Zeus that brought Hephaestus
to Hera: the God of Fire
and he was ablaze
with a fiery passion
from the beginning of his life.

Not the peaceful Vulcan he was perceived as,
he bound his mother
to a cursed throne,
fury igniting in his mind
and guiding his scolding hands.

With molten lava and iron,
he killed the giant Mimas:
a brief repose
for the magma
mounting inside of him.

It was Zeus who ordered Hephaestus
to create Pandora from Earth
and from water
a fair seedling
with talents endowed upon her

from the Gods of music,
persuasion

and beauty
with the four winds' breath
bringing her to life,

his appetite raged in a blaze,
his fires glowed until he burned:
a desire for possession
- a destiny of destruction,

those restless, searing hands grasped
in a midst of salacious spite
that stung
as he struggled to take her as his own.

Amid Pandora's prying,
her release
of all evil,
eradication of hope
and thus,
resulting rejection,

Hephaestus boiled close beneath the surface.

Those abhorrent hands
blistering with lust
and the yearning to
just
touch

tried to hold the
licking flames down,
out of sight,
but they surged up and out
with swelling force,
up
through charred fingers

and out.

Tele-who?

I am the one forgotten;
when my father is wrapped
in a beautiful Goddess
when my mother is weeping
for days and nights

in her bedroom
when the maids are weaving
and washing:
I am the one forgotten.

What makes a mother?

A protector, a kind word, a soft touch,
or soft alone?
When all you are
is being butchered and bludgeoned
by a hundred or more suitors

Where was my mother then?
Was she crying in bed?
Or was she weaving with maids?
With maids: women who take my mother's place
who bathe and feed me

Perhaps they did not deserve to die
perhaps they were to blame
for how I am
perhaps, perhaps

perhaps my mother deserved to die

for leaving me
to cower in the corner
of what was once a home.

Was it ever told that I went to find
My father? Did you hear that?

I went and I searched, Piraeus
and Theoclymenus accompanied me, but
they bore no interest
in the search itself.

Instead they wished to find the Goddesses,
sirens using their wiles,
postponing my father's return.

Upon reaching Eumaeus' hut
my father disposed of his disguise
and never did a more
glorious sight
move me so:
My Hero.

Together we planned the return to the palace –
the disguise and the slaughter:
the suitors died
the maids died

Even my father was killed once
but at the overwrought hand

of Telegonus
he was bestowed with immortality
as was my mother
and as was I.

Naturally I am the one forgotten;
when all is done
and not at all said
when death is upon
everyone but me
I am the one forgotten.

Tartarus

Before Hades – the unseen one – ruled the Underworld,
presiding over death and the dead
with a bird-tipped sceptre and a cornucopia of fertility.
There was Tartarus.

Beyond the barriers of dusk,
surpassing the dense walls of bronze,
an eighteen day fall from the heavens,
at the very end of the world.
There lies Tartarus.

An eternal tomb of distress
where storms seethe and your most reticent fears
are exercised for recreation.
This is Tartarus.

Endnotes

Atlas — the Titan leading the rebellion against Zeus was eventually cursed by Zeus himself, to hold the world on his back for eternity. By use of Medusa's head, he was turned into the Atlas Mountains. He was father to the three groups of women: Hesperides, Pleiades, and Hyades. The Hyades had a brother, Hyas, who was killed, the tears of the Hyades were said to bring rain to Earth. In a moment of compassion, Zeus turned them into the Hyades star cluster which make up the Taurus constellation (shown on the cover).

Apollo — the God of music (often found playing a golden lyre) sought to keep Cassandra as his own, in order to win her, he gave her powers of prophecy, yet when she rejected him, he cursed her to be constantly seen as a liar.

Echo — the Oreiad nymph, was cursed by Hera to only ever be able to repeat the last few words someone says. Unable to approach anyone first, she lived a lonely life, until she fell in love with Narcissus. Narcissus rejects her advances, falling in love with himself instead, and Echo's body dies, only leaving her mind and echoing voice.

Eris (also known as Discordia) — Goddess of strife, discord, contention and rivalry, often haunted the battlefields. Her resentment comes from her not being invited to Thetis and Peleus' wedding. When she turned up, however, she threw a golden apple at the guests; the apple had 'to the fairest' written upon it and, in desperation to be declared the fairest, three goddesses fought over it, causing the events which led to the Trojan War.

*Persephone [pər'sɛfəni: / puh-**seh**-fuh-nee]* — Goddess of the Underworld and Spring, was once abducted by Hades in order to become his bride. When her mother Demeter stormed the Underworld to bring her back, Hades agreed to let Persephone live above ground for half of the year (Spring and Summer) and forced her to stay with him underground for Autumn and Winter.

*Eurydice [jʊə'rɪdɪsi: / yoo-**ri**-duh-see]* — who was sent to the Underworld when she died of snake poison, was to be rescued by her husband Orpheus. Hades, under Orpheus' charms, allowed Eurydice to leave the Underworld under one condition – Orpheus was not to look back until he was in direct sunlight.

There are three members of *The Fates* — Clotho, she who spins the thread of life, Lachesis *[lækɪsɪs / **la**-kuh-suhs]*, she who measures the length of life and choses how it shall be lived and finally, Atropos *[ætrəpəs / **ah**-truh-puhs]*, who cuts the thread of life at the time of death.

*Hephaestus [hɪ'fi:stəs / huh-**fee**-stuhs]* — God of Fire, was typically seen as kind, but there are several myths told where he has shown fury and impatience. I chose to examine the darker, less familiar side of the God.

*Telemachus [tə 'lɛməkəs / tuh-**leh**-muh-kuhs]*— Son of Odysseus and Penelope, spent most of his adulthood searching Sparta for his father, following the Trojan War.

Tartarus — A region of the Underworld, where the worst criminals and creatures would reside.

Printed in Great Britain
by Amazon